Bod's
Dream

Michael and Joanne Cole

EGMONT

EGMONT

We bring stories to life

Original hardback edition first published in Great Britain 1965 by Methuen & Co. Ltd.
This edition first published in Great Britain 2015 by Egmont UK Limited,
The Yellow Building, 1 Nicholas Road, London W11 4AN
www.egmont.co.uk

Endpaper and cover design by Lo Cole

ISBN 978 1 4052 7588 0

A CIP catalogue record for this title is available from the British Library.

Stay safe online. Egmont is not responsible for content hosted by third parties.

MIX
Paper from
responsible sources
FSC® C018306

Here's Bod in bed. He's having a lovely dream. In the dream he's eating a large bowl of strawberries and cream.

Next morning he can think of nothing but strawberries and cream. When he goes out he's still in a dream about them, and doesn't look where he's going.

Along comes Frank the postman with a letter for Bod.

"Mornin', Bod," says Frank.

But Bod doesn't see or hear him.

He's in such a daydream about the strawberries he wouldn't have noticed if an elephant had been the postman.

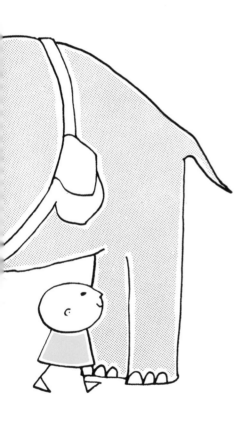

"That's funny," says Frank.
"What can Bod be thinking
about?" And he's so curious
to know that he can't help
following him.

They pass Farmer Barleymow on his tractor.

"Mornin'," says Barleymow.

But they walk by without answering him.

Bod's so busy thinking about strawberries, and Frank's so busy thinking about what Bod can be thinking about . . .

. . . they wouldn't have noticed if Farmer Barleymow had been a scarecrow.

"Well, I never!" says Barleymow.
And full of wonder, he follows them.

Soon they come to Aunt Flo.

"Good morning, everybody," says Aunt Flo.

But they're all so busy with their own thoughts
that they walk past without answering her.

They wouldn't have noticed her if she had been standing on her head.

"What can they be up to?" says Aunt Flo.
And lost in thought, she follows them.

By and by they come to a hole in the ground.

Bod doesn't see it. He's dreaming of strawberries.

He walks straight into the hole – and disappears.

Frank is so busy thinking about what Bod can be
thinking about . . .

. . . that he doesn't even notice that Bod has disappeared. He, too, walks into the hole.

And Barleymow is so busy thinking about what Bod and Frank can be thinking about . . .

. . . that he doesn't see the hole either.

Nor does Aunt Flo.

Then along comes P.C. Copper. He sees the hole.

"That's a dangerous hole," he says. "Someone might fall down it."

So he puts up signs saying 'Stop, Danger,'

and directs people away from the hole.

Suddenly he hears voices coming from the hole. "Hello, hello," he says, shining his torch. "Anybody down there?"

"Yes," says Bod. "And guess what we've found down here?"

"Umm . . . umm . . . I give up," says P.C. Copper.

"An enormous bowl of strawberries and cream!
Just like I dreamt about. Come and join us!"

"Can't eat on duty," says P.C. Copper.
"Save me a strawberry for later."

When they come up, Bod says goodbye to his
friends and gives P.C. Copper his strawberry.
"Pop it under my helmet," says P.C. Copper.
Then Bod walks off in another happy dream.